CAMPER CATASTROPHE

By Mary Lu Scholl

ISBN-13:9781729593134
ISBN-10:1729593135

DEDICATION

This is dedicated to my friends and family and fans who read my books with love and tolerance.

CONTENTS

ACKNOWLEDGMENTS

Thank you to Wikipedia!

Also thank you to the many authors whom I would name but it might embarrass them to be called my role models!

There are also a number of people who might imagine they see themselves in my stories; not so. While some situations or opinions may apply to them, situations or opinions are common to many people and unless I have your permission or even your request, no one I know is represented in my books.

CHAPTER 1

NEW LIFE

It was my first night in the trailer park and I was having trouble going to sleep. My animals were unsettled. Birds screeched and I wondered what fauna dramas were unfolding. Were they angry, defending their territory, or dying? Mating was out of the question, noises like that couldn't promote procreation. On that thought, a feral cat screeched, unmistakably in heat.

I was just flat unhappy. I crawled out of the bed trying not to disturb my cats, who had finally fallen asleep in impossible positions. Standing in front of the window in the kitchen any passersby could see me in my nightgown. The blinds were closed in the bedroom area, but the rest were open for light – and to relieve the inevitable claustrophobia of a travel trailer, should anyone visit who suffered from that particular malady; like me. (What was I thinking?) Maybe I should shut all of the blinds; but that would be a pain in the rear, with belongings everywhere around the edges. Storage was at a premium in my new shoebox house.

This from a woman who didn't even care about shoes.

At least I didn't have any ghosts around. My late husbands hadn't "seen the light" and gone on right away, like they were supposed to. With Don it may have been concern for me. With George it was probably because he knew Don was around. It had been disconcerting at first, both times. I hadn't seen either of them since I moved down here. I don't know that much about ghosts and they neither one condescended to explain, or even talk to me. Maybe they were tied to a place or an object and I was now out of their reach. I'm pretty sure they're the only ones I've seen; but how would I know if the person on the street corner was alive or not? I also know that no one around me could see either of them – at least not when around me. Trust me, I looked plenty crazy a few times.

I stepped over my big cocker spaniel, Buddy, to get to the bathroom and tripped over the cat litter. Okay, that didn't work, it had to go somewhere else. I moved the trash to a small counter, it had to be out of Buddy's reach or he would spread it everywhere when left alone. Then the purse and keys would have to go….there. The basket with the household crap that accumulates (change, batteries, receipts…)(why do I save those little packets of silica gel?) could go on the far end of the banquette, no one sits back there anyway, and the cat litter could go by the bathroom door.

Buddy scratched at the door and I winced at the damage it would do to the little screen. Opening the door and peeking out to see if there was anyone there, all I could see was shadows. Good, I didn't have to look for my teeth. He pulled on his short leash over to the grassy area designated as my yard. A squirrel jumped onto one of those huge balls of plants hung from the neighbor's tree. Orchids? Ferns? They rocked gently at the ends of their chains. I could just see the huge shape – about the size of a lumpy green and tan beach ball.

I hadn't turned on any lights so I wouldn't even try to pick up any poop. I could get it in the morning; it was in my yard anyway. A cat squealed from somewhere on the next street over and another dog barked from somewhere. It sounded like a bigger dog; maybe my North Neighbor's black lab.

I tugged on Buddy's leash to get his attention away from whatever had scampered under the trailer while he pooped. Probably a rat. I had hardly hung up his leash and turned to latch the door when I saw a light moving back and forth across the driveway that led to the four trailers in my little cul-de-sac. Did one of my ghosts find me? Nah, it was just a flashlight. What the hell? It was three in the morning!

It was still early morning when I went out with Buddy and picked up the poop from earlier in the morning. I seriously missed dog doors. Maybe there's a way I could block the porch off. That vinyl lattice across the trailer side…No, then he would poop on the concrete. Also, the cats would get out.

I know, there are all kinds of cats outside in Florida, but mine were raised in an urban environment. They understood cars, not carnivores. Patches had already gotten a bad rash from somewhere. It seemed like every time I picked her up I was torturing her with either pills that tasted bad or an ointment that, I suspected, stung and tasted even worse.

I was tired, but then I was always tired lately. I had started sleeping with the lights on at night when my ghosts started showing up at night – they didn't like the lights. Even though I hadn't seen them recently I still tried to sleep with the lights on. The lights in the trailer, along with the cooler and refrigerator, though, were erratic. They just turned themselves off and back on a minute or two later; the flickering would wake me; one more irritation.

Right up there with the sugar ants.

I fixed my favorite breakfast, scrambled eggs with peppers and cheese but wasn't quite done eating when the alarm went off, reminding me to log on to an on-line writing seminar. This was going to be my life from now on. I would write mysteries to supplement my income and occupy whatever time I had left in this world. I amended that. I would write until my son came to his senses, married a nice fertile woman, moved back down here and gave me grandchildren. I picked out the peppers from the last of the eggs and ate them, sliding the rest into

Buddy's bowl.

The dark screen waited for the designated time to start and it reflected my face, unfortunately. At least it wasn't an interactive course where I would have to turn on the laptop camera and have everyone look at me when I had to respond. I look like a toad without my teeth in. A gray haired toad with thick psychedelic pink eyeglasses. Well so what? It's not like I'm trying to attract attention, especially from a man. I've been married four times. That's enough for anyone.

"I just aim at not frightening small children." I muttered to myself.

The confident face of literary excellence flickered onto my screen.

CHAPTER 2

NEW NEIGHBOR

So, basically, it boiled down to write what you know and to self-publish in today's market.

Pay a marketer instead of an agent.

Evaluate what you like to read – that obviously sells; you bought it, now write it!

E:books are the wave of the future. Thousands of books are uploaded to Amazon every DAY. There are more than 30,000 romance authors alone; of course, that genre was the most diverse when you consider you can find romance anywhere. Violence, sex, mysteries or even science fiction.

So my next book will be a sexy mystery. I'm not sure I remember enough about sex to be realistic. On the other hand, was sex ever realistic?

Maybe another serial killer book.

Truth-be-told, I was really getting tired of serial killers. All the new books seemed to be trying to one-up each other by getting gorier, more violent or just flat more weird. I almost hated to admit I had contributed there, but mine wasn't THAT bad; my readers just needed to avoid Halloween Haunted Houses for a while.

The trouble with going back to read familiar authors and books from years ago was that I had read so much that it seemed like half the books I picked up at the library or downloaded on Kindle looked interesting at first but within the first chapter I would know I had already read them.

I decided to carry my laptop out onto the patio. Backing out the door with my hands full I heard the crunch of golf-cart tires. The lack of engine noise was a little disconcerting. The golf carts were cute, though. I looked and it was the maintenance guy who had been so helpful when I first set up. I hurriedly checked with my tongue to see if my top teeth were in.

Pete; that was his name. "Good morning, Pete."

A good looking guy, a little on the stocky side, he had his cat on the seat beside him. He stopped his golden cart with the pick-up bed attachment on the back and smiled.

Why would he smile at me? Was my shirt on inside out?

"Good morning, Miss!"

I hadn't gotten used to that form of address, either. I'm a widow, twice actually, and had been single now for a few years, but "Miss" didn't seem to fit. My son said it was just a generic form of address in southern speech, respectful.

"Say, do you know about anyone wandering around in the middle of the night with a flashlight?"

"Well," he seemed to consider my question seriously, "there isn't a curfew, you know. It is a little unusual, though, unless someone was walking a dog. Was there a dog?"

"I don't think so." I'd have to stick with that answer or look like an idiot since that's why I had been out there.

"Can you describe the person?"

"No, it was dark."

"There's a security light just over there." He gestured with a cigarette. "There's another one at the end of the drive, by the way. You might watch to see if you can get a better look at him if he comes again and moves closer to one of them. I'll ask some of the other guys if they know who it may have been."

I nodded. "Thank you, I would appreciate it. I'm still not accustomed to being alone." Strange as it may seem, I even felt safe with my husbands' ghosts around; their absence was unsettling. Buddy was a watch dog, he would just watch whomever it was. My cats? Ashes may be more dangerous than Buddy, and .she was declawed

"We're pretty safe here, and you have neighbors who have been here a long time, but if you need anything or get frightened at night you can call me. Do you still have the receipt from when you moved in? My number is on that; and I'm just over on the next road."

It occurred to me later that I could have given a more gracious response than a grunt of acknowledgment to his offer. Had I ever had any people skills? Probably not.

"Mrs. Decker?"

Buddy and I were sitting on the patio, surrounded on two sides by a 6 foot wooden fence and the trailer itself on the third. I had crammed it full of plants, each placed for optimum shade or sun. The voice was from the open, south side where my little truck was parked. One of the neighbors stood there with his lab on a leash. The North Neighbor, as I thought of him when I couldn't remember his name. Come on, I was still new. Had nothing to do with my being an unsociable bitch. I grimaced at remembering that review of a speech I had given – I had ducked out immediately after. Social I'm not.

"Yeah." I looked up but didn't make an effort to be friendly.

"Pete said you saw someone with a flashlight last night. It was probably just old Albert. If he hears someone open or shut their door really late he assumes someone is turning their dog out to poop on the road so he goes out to look for it with his flashlight." He gave an abashed chuckle at my expression. "I don't think he ever sleeps. Since I was the one closest with a dog until you got here, he would pick it up with a bag and leave it on the stair to my trailer for me to step on it accidentally when I get up."

I looked at him, incredulous. "You're serious?"

"Yeah. He's harmless; just a pain in the...butt." He now looked definitely guilty.

"I guess I let my dog loose one time too many and he's been getting even now for months. I only rarely let her out without me anymore; only if I'm sick, say, but he goes out and looks anyway."

"Which one is Albert?" I was staring from trailer to mobile home to trailer, trying to identify where the jerk lived.

"He's the one in the thirty foot Coachman at the end of the driveway by the green singlewide."

I narrowed my eyes. "By the bird people?"

The bird people had a screen room running the length of their trailer. It had huge cages inside along the screen side, shaded by a variety of flowering vines that alternately impressed me and made me feel claustrophobic just looking at them.

"The Jaxsons', yeah."

The quiet lasted too long for him to imagine I was going to invite him to join me, so he shuffled his feet and repeated his information. He was bald and a little heavy, had that body type that suggests diabetes – top or bottom heavy, a little out of proportion. He smiled at me. "I just didn't want you to worry; wanted you to know it was just him." He gathered his dog's leash closer and tugged. They meandered down the driveway.

I suppose I could have asked him to sit, his legs were swollen and he probably had trouble standing any length of time. Trouble was, why would he want to? Then he would just have to talk to me.

I locked Buddy in the trailer with the cats since it was too hot to leave him in the truck any length of time, and headed to the county library to borrow a few DVDs.

Several Agatha Christie, Sherlock Holmes and a few other classics later, I was humming as I turned back down the driveway.

The man who had to be Albert was sitting on his open porch drinking a beer and reading a foreign newspaper of some kind. We hadn't actually met, or maybe I just hadn't noticed him until now. I stopped my truck and rolled the passenger window down.

"I'll have you know I pick up my own dog's poop!" I gunned the motor and yanked to the left. Rolling the window up would have been too slow for emphasis, so I parked the truck between the two of us and exited hastily; hoping to unlock my door and get inside before he tried to answer.

I could roll the window up later sometime before two; (that being the time the rain invariably came down in buckets).

Righteous anger expended, I was then

somewhat aghast at my own temerity. Slamming the door behind me startled both cats. Ashes rolled over too fast and fell out of the bottom bunk reserved for her use. Patches blinked enormous and fearful eyes from her nest in the shared bed.

A bottle of water and stroking my animals gave my hands something to do while I obsessively went over the interaction again and again, changing words and refining actions way too long after the fact to have any purpose. I saw again his shock at the tirade wash over his rather patrician face. His spare frame and erect posture irritated me because it was so contrary to my more of a mashed potato shape. I made myself stop my pointless perseveration and retreated to my bed, hiding behind drawn blinds.

I fumbled to open the plastic case to the DVD, agitation making my hand shake, and popped it into the DVD player. As a matter of habit I grabbed the clicker and turned the sound up to 100. I really needed to get hearing aids.

I didn't want to.

The rumble of war planes emanated from the open window that night as John Wayne carried the country to victory in one of his military films; thrilling both me and Maureen O'Hara.

It must have been about midnight when there was a knock. I thought I heard the crunch of tires over the sound of the movie, but sometimes the guy at the very far end came and went late. I sat up, unsure if I really heard the sound.

"Hello? Ma'am, can you hear me?" There was another knock.

I punched pause and scrambled out of bed, waking up Buddy from his gentle snoring by accidentally stepping on him.

He didn't hear any better than I did.

"Coming." I peered across my diminutive sink and out the small kitchen window. "What do you want?"

A very nice young man's face appeared through the glass and he asked me again to answer the door. I caught a glimpse of his green uniform and then saw the white cruiser parked behind my truck.

"Just a minute." I pulled a robe off the hook on the bathroom door.

"What do you want?" I didn't care if I came across as a curmudgeon, it was the middle of the damn night. "Is this about the prowler last night?"

I stepped out of the door, checked to make sure the latch had opened properly, pulled the dog-cat gate across to discourage the cats from following, told Buddy to be good and lie back down. Then I shut the door gently, the whole process slowed down to a crawl to emphasize just how inconvenient the hour was.

I found myself staring at the middle button on his shirt. Just how tall was this kid? I backed up and hit my ankle on the metal stair, swearing and putting out a hand to catch myself. "Back up, damn it. You're too tall for your own good."

The Deputy backed up a couple of steps and I nearly fell again. Naturally; I had grabbed his arm for balance and didn't let go fast enough. He steadied me with his other hand but let go quickly.

Deputy C. Johnson refrained from smiling.

He had a baby face. Probably thought looking friendly took away some of his authority. His mustache was struggling, but would probably make him look older…someday.

He refrained from smiling because his mama would take a stick to him for being rude. This little woman was a spitfire; she reminded him of his own grandmother, except for the long stringy gray hair. His grandmother had hers in the ubiquitous curly cap of the genteel older, southern woman.

"I'm sorry Ma'am. We had a complaint about noise coming from your trailer. Now that I'm here I can tell you I recognized the movie, and I don't think it was particularly excessive, but then I'm not trying to sleep only a few feet from your window, either."

He paused. "I like that movie, by the way; but not everyone can tolerate gunfire late at night and in the dark. The caller mentioned that he suffers from PTSD and wants you to shut the windows, wear ear buds or turn it down."

I opened my mouth to reply and realized I didn't have my teeth in and would have a lisp. That pissed me off even more. "Am I so frightening he can't tell me himself?" *How scary can an old toad woman with a lisp be, anyway?*

"I don't think so." The officer grinned. Now, he grinned. "However, he mentioned a confrontation earlier in the day with you, and then said he thought you had a man here and he didn't want to start a fight."

It had to be Albert, then. I was more irritated at the inference that there was a man inside than that I played my movie too loud.

"I assure you, the only man's voice he may have heard was John Wayne's, and if he doesn't recognize that voice he must be a communist. Or he's a terrorist, I guess that's the modern appellation."

"Appe…" The young man hesitated.

"Just a name." He must have gone to school in West Virginia.

There was a spate of numbers rumbling out of his radio. He clicked a button and replied in the same numeric code. "I think we're okay here; you'll turn it down a little?" He backed away quickly and headed back to his car. "Thank you, Ma'am."

So now I decided I like "Miss" better. I fumbled with the latch, hoping I wouldn't have to get at the spare key I had hidden. The door had clicked shut behind me once. Now I had five sets of the keys; one thoroughly hidden on the porch. The door swung open and I met three sets of concerned eyes. They loved me. My heart softened and I tiredly went inside. The movie was over anyway.

The next time I went to the library I

was going to look for The Guns of Navarone.

CHAPTER 3

NEW FRIEND

I stared at the keyboard. It didn't move. I knew a little about a lot of things but not a lot about anything. Except caring for people who just die on you anyway.

My third husband had died of congestive heart failure. It was a long, miserable way to die, and the process had started long before I married him. He was much older and I had cared for him a long time before I lost him. He had stuck around for quite a while – but didn't speak. He faded a little and I rarely saw him after I married again.

My last husband indulged in cigarettes and tequila (the good stuff)… and beer… and rum. He drank himself to death. He had warned me when we first met that he didn't ever plan on being 60; but I hadn't taken it seriously. Twelve years later he was 59. I had been caring for him as he carelessly fulfilled his own prophecy. He was an angry ghost and rattled and made noise. He would pop in and scare me on purpose. He's been gone quite a while now. I think I mentioned I haven't seen either one of them since I moved down here.

Honestly, I was glad to have been there for both, but didn't want to do it again. I had moved to Florida to be in warm weather and be near my son.

He promptly moved. "Nothing personal." He said.

To be fair, he had asked me to move with him but I chose warmth.

Should I write about caregiving? No, don't even want to go there, even in print. No mysteries there, either.

There was a sudden commotion on the other side of my truck somewhere. I couldn't see what was going on until I got up and peeked over. It was a loud squawking from the doublewide with the birds and a string of cuss words from, apparently, an unhappy bird. Raised voices, one from inside the house (Mrs. Jaxson?) and a man's from the road, took over as the bird abruptly stopped.

Voices carried but not the words.

What the heck, I didn't have anything else to do. I snatched up the small bag of trash by the door, grabbed Buddy's leash (with him attached) and headed for the commotion. I got to the edge of my concrete and had to turn back to grab my upper denture and stick it in my mouth.

"...can't even enjoy a coffee on his own porch without some blasted bird cussing at him!"

An improbably red coiffure bobbed as a short, skinny woman in a voluminous tropical dress of some kind tried to defend her foul-mouthed fowl. She even looked a little like a bird, maybe a Sandhill Crane.

"But Mr. Cross, he only cusses at you, and only when he catches you looking at him. I'll move his cage to the other end of the porch; but he'll still see you when you walk to the community hall. Maybe if you spoke kindly..."

Apparently Albert's last name was Cross, appropriate; and I was not the only one who didn't like him. I had the dubious distinction of sharing my opinion with a Grey Parrot.

My neighbor was storming back to his own space when I passed him, and I giggled all the way to the community dumpster. There were one hundred and three steps to the dumpster, and I enjoyed all two hundred and six steps of the errand.

There was supposed to be Bingo that night at the community center. I really wanted to go, just for something different. I wanted to meet some of the women who lived here. I had played Bingo as a kid but wasn't sure if this was the same.

The thin walls of the trailer were closing in on me. I really had to go.

I picked my way down the driveway and ninety-seven steps to the community hall. I had peeked in but not spent any time here yet. There was an exercise area. There were more than a dozen tables and chairs. There were bookshelves crammed with everything from DVDs (!) books, puzzles and games. One corner was a very respectably appointed kitchen, brimming with snacks.

Well, I could bring some next time. I loved cooking. If it's rich or fattening, I can do it. I sniffed appreciatively as I entered the tiled corner. None of it was on my self-imposed diet, but what the heck. It's not like I was ever really going to be slim, anyway.

I ignored the curious glances and outright stares from the occupied tables and stopped at the check-in. I bought my cards and picked up a red dauber.

I settled one seat away from another woman sitting alone. I was far enough away she could ignore me, but I could see what she was doing.

I was admiring her Tiger's Eye jewelry mixed in with the other chains and the ceramic bangles when she smiled at me. "I'm Muriel."

I smiled back. "I'm Patricia Decker." It occurred to me that was the first time I had introduced myself with my first name since settling in. It didn't matter, I thought cynically, by tomorrow everyone in the park would know my name and that I had gone to Bingo. Southern state, small town and smaller park.

The caller was obviously experienced and I had to pay attention to keep up. Muriel bingoed once but I donated to the cause, or paid for the pleasure, however you wanted to look at it.

As we gathered up stuff to go home, several women spoke to me and said it was good that I came.

What else could they say? On the other hand, they didn't have to speak to at all. I was going to have to get rid of this chip on my shoulder it suddenly occurred to me. I really was a bitch.

Muriel trailed after me. I tried to decide to be nice or not, I wanted a friend but didn't need another puppy. She didn't *really* look like an apricot poodle; and we probably just lived the same direction.

However, I had to admit, I was lonely. It wouldn't hurt me to talk to her. Besides she looked like she liked crafts – her bingo bag looked home-made, and she may have made her jewelry. If she didn't do such things herself, she clearly appreciated them.

"You just moved in next to Mr. Cross, didn't you? He's such a nice man. He loves my muffins."

There went that relationship. As soon

as she broached the subject of his new neighbor with him, I was going to be mud.

"Yes. He and I have not actually had a conversation yet." There, that was true. I can bluff with the best. "We'll have to get together – do you play Rummicube?"

"I love it! My late husband used to play with me all the time." She got out her phone to get my number, I obliged and she called it so I would have hers.

"He died of cancer two years ago." She added.

Well that's a conversation stopper this time of night. "I'm sorry for your loss."

She scurried off to the northwest end of the park. I headed…southeast…of course.

Mary Lu Scholl

CHAPTER 4

NEW MYSTERY

The next morning I was, once again, attending to canine nature, when I glanced over and saw Nathan (I remembered the North Neighbor's name that morning. He was hanging tightly onto Dog's leash. (Okay, I remembered Nathan, do you expect me to remember the dog as well?)

"Albert! Hey Albert!" Nathan was standing nearby Albert's deck and calling our neighbor's name.

Albert was seated at his outdoor table with his paper. His head was down on the crumpled paper. One hand dangled loosely, the other still held one edge of the newsprint. I looped Buddy's leash over a handy two-by-four sticking up by my porch and went over when Albert didn't stir.

Nathan had his phone out and was dialing 911, I assumed. I stepped up onto enemy territory and shook Albert's shoulder to see if we could get a response. His eyes were open, blue, and staring past me at…nothing. His skin had a tinge of blue. I got very close to see if he was breathing. I could see every pore on his face, but nothing moved, flared or reacted to me. He smelled of Old Spice Aftershave, with chocolate, coffee and cherries, coconut and almonds; with a touch of bile.

I may not see very well, or hear very well, but I do have a keen sense of smell! I didn't touch him, I backed slowly off the cedar planks that supported the PVC furniture and the unfortunate Mr. Cross. I tripped, naturally, and fell, the rip-rap driveway abrading my right knee. "I think he's dead." Nathan stepped back in distaste and raised his phone to his ear. Then I turned back to my own trailer to take Buddy inside and wipe the blood off my knee.

My phone was sitting on the table by my computer. It was open to the many-times-started-and-many-times-changed first page of my next novel.

Hey, a mystery, at least at the moment! Okay, that reaction is a little cold, I had to admit it to myself, but it wasn't as if I liked the man.

Pulling up my camera app, I almost fell again in my hurry to get back outside. Nathan still stood in the drive holding his phone. If I didn't want to look like a ghoul I had to get rid of him.

"Nathan, the ambulance will never find us – you know we aren't GPS friendly back here; why don't you walk to the end of the driveway. I'll call the manager and let him know what's happening."

Nathan agreed and spoke to whoever was talking to him at the call center. He headed toward the end of the drive where it met an actual hard road.

I jumped back up on the porch and started taking pictures. I got the body from several angles, the table, the newspaper and what he must have been reading. A plate with a half-eaten muffin on it. A paper cup from the coffee shop, almost empty, set just far enough away that it hadn't been tipped when Albert collapsed. The solid door to his trailer was open, just the screen was closed. I took a quick glance toward Nathan. He was facing away from me, toward the access road the emergency vehicle would be coming up.

His dog, however, looked back at me with suspicion.

I moved to Albert's steps and stuck my phone in the door, clicked numerous pictures in several different directions. I hastily beat a retreat when I caught a glimpse of lights from the ambulance as it went by in front of the mobile homes directly behind my neighbors and me. Belatedly, I glanced over at the bird-people's house to see if anyone was watching me behave with something less than circumspection. None of the birds were out yet that I could see.

The few of us standing around and volunteering information to the EMTs and police didn't get much in return from them.

Our general consensus at first was that

he had a heart attack. Someone snickered and opined that meant he had one.

Bad manners, that; to say out loud what we all were thinking.

Nathan, who apparently had better hearing than most of us said the ME had ruled the heart attack out in a preliminary report to the deputy on duty. It wasn't my deputy. This one, Boatright, his name tag said, had character lines between bushy eyebrows. The gray in his golden head of hair added depth, but it also gave him maturity. He had the age and carriage of some seniority and experience; too much of both to be sent out to yell at an old lady at the behest of an old man.

Under his direction several underlings gathered up everything that was loose on the porch and carried off a tote full of things from inside. Deputy Boatright put orange tape around the entire site and used a key from a hook by Albert's door to lock the trailer up tight.

He took statements from Nathan and me, separately. I couldn't hear anything they said over on Nathan's porch while I waited on my own.

I don't know about Nathan for sure, but he seems like a much nicer person than I am; so his statement was probably not very helpful.

As for me, I was raised not to speak ill of the dead, so the department was on their own. Other neighbors I had not yet met waited their turn to talk after a reporter showed up and started shoving a microphone at people and snapping pictures.

Belatedly I remembered to call the manager. I called Pete just for good measure.

Mary Lu Scholl

CHAPTER 5

NEW LEAF

The first thing I did was move all the pictures I had taken over to my laptop. From there I logged onto Walgreens and uploaded the whole bunch, paid for double prints, 4 x 6 matte, and ordered them for pick-up in an hour.

I spent that hour at Walmart buying

bribery staples like chocolate, sugar, flour and eggs, nuts, sprinkles and butter.

I hadn't been there long enough to have my own spot on the local grapevine, or be part of their park's information web. So I decided to rectify that. Food gets you in anywhere, even if you are a bitch. I needed to establish my niche – as a welcome guest and maybe not quite so anti-social as I apparently appeared to be.

I thought I showed remarkable constraint when I got home (grimace) and mixed up a batch of peanut butter brownies before I even opened the envelope of pictures. I considered the exercise to be character building.

When the timer was set and Ashes on my lap, Patches peeking out of the recess by the door that I had lined in fleece the first time I found her hiding there, a 24-ounce-recycled-V8-bottle of water in front of me, I finally opened the flap on the picture envelope.

As the color photos spilled out onto the table I relived the taking of them. There was the exhilaration of doing something clandestine, but also the natural repugnance of death and, for me, curiosity, all vying for top billing.

"Hello?"

I jumped and Ashes disappeared in a tornado of gray fur. I regretted that. Patches seemed to get far more attention lately, albeit repugnant attention, medicine, etcetera.

My first thought was that it was only when I wanted to be alone that I got company. Have to work on that reaction, turn over a new leaf.

"Hi, Muriel." I scooped the pictures back into the envelope and invited her in.

"I'll have brownies in…" I glanced at the timer "three minutes. I have water or root beer flavored water if you'd like."

I stopped to see what her response would be and really looked at her for the first time. Her face was ravaged by grief. She wasn't crying now, but she had been. I wondered if she had come over to our alley for the comfort of being near Albert's place. She had apparently underestimated her response to the locked and taped trailer. I knew they had been friends, now it was obvious there had been more.

I certainly understood. I put one hand over hers and asked what I could do. My son would have been proud.

That was all it took, tears spilled over again. She pulled out a handkerchief (*who carries those today?*) and I saw an AC embroidered on one corner. Well, that answered that. I wondered if she had done the embroidery. It was really very well done. French knots and chain stitches in green.

"I just needed to come over and see for myself. My neighbors didn't tell me and I didn't know until the manager knocked on my door a little while ago. I even brought some more of his muffins just in case everyone was wrong or I misunderstood."

The timer on the brownies went off and I jumped up to get them out. I was alternately appalled at her neighbors and still understood why they would avoid the responsibility. It was obvious even to me, a stranger and newbie, how close they were.

She was carrying a paper sack with what was apparently more of the same muffin batch she had already shared with Albert. "Have the detectives talked to you yet?"

She sniffed once more. "No. I was going to call them. I feel like I'm the next of kin, but I know he had a daughter somewhere in the west. They didn't get on; he never saw her and rarely heard from her." She set the sack down on the table out of her way.

"You should call them and volunteer whatever they might want."

"I suppose so; now that I've seen for myself that it's true." She raised her brimming eyes to me once more. "There's no doubt? He's really not at the hospital instead?" The powder on her face had mostly rubbed off. Her lipstick was all over the handkerchief. But as naked as her face was, her pretty light blue eyes were more so as they implored me to tell her he was in the intensive care unit at whatever the closest hospital was. (I had no idea, hadn't needed to know that, yet.) I did know, however, that Albert was dead. I had pictorial evidence only inches from her. For a second I considered showing her, fortunately the impulse passed.

"I was there. He's gone. I'm sorry. Is there someone else you should call? Do you have children or a sibling nearby?"

"No." She said sadly. "Just me left; my Carroll and I didn't have children." She fingered the pretty onyx necklace that hung low on top of her sleeveless tunic. It matched the black drops in her ears. Even as patchy as her make-up was, it looked better than any I had ever worn.

I offered her the card Detective Boatright had left with me. She pulled out one of those Jitterbug phones and wiggled her fingers in front of Patches while she dialed.

I only heard her side of the conversation but gathered that she was going to meet him at her home in a little while.

I sent her off with a brownie thinking maybe we really could be friends.

I eyed the bottle of water from the refrigerator. I was behind on my ounces. I gulped the rest of the bottle and Buddy caught my eye as I put it in the sink to refill. Sure enough, his bowl had reduced to a wet patch. I moved it to a more prominent but less convenient location and wondered just how long it was going to take to have a place for everything and everything in its place.

As Buddy thirstily lapped, Patches peered out from under the cabinet I left open for her. Sure enough, it was time to torture her again. I bribed her out with a couple of cat treats and picked her up; she turned boneless and let me drag her across my lap. I crushed the awful pill and mixed it with a bit of soft butter, praying she would lap it up. She had, for a while; then she must have figured out why it tasted funny. I regretfully wiped it on her fur so she would have to lick it off, and then held her firmly to spread the cream on her back.

She disappeared immediately when I let go. Now I had a ghost cat.

Since I would have to clean off the table before getting back into the pictures, I might as well eat supper first. A peanut butter sandwich sufficed and I was ready to try again.

I had to wonder why I was so willing to procrastinate with looking at the pictures. This many hours later my adrenaline had worn off. Was my stomach really queasy at the thought of the pictures? It was probably a good thing I didn't stop to think before I did stuff like take those pictures; I'd never have any fun.

Mary Lu Scholl

CHAPTER 6

NEW INFORMATION

No more procrastinating. Everyone was fed. I switched on the light that was plugged into an outlet so I knew it would stay on.

The pictures spilled onto the table again.

What did I know about solving mysteries? What did I even know about recognizing a mystery? I sorted the pictures by category starting with the body.

It was unnerving, looking at him again. I had only really been face-to-face with him once, and not up close, ever, until the pictures.

To be entirely fair, I had started our discord, and had based it on hearsay from a neighbor with affirmation from a parrot. In retrospect, I had, perhaps, been a bit hasty in judgement.

He was an attractive man for his age, which wasn't much older than me, actually. Too bad he had been so aggravating. The close-up picture of his face and picture of the position of his body seemed intrusive.

Hell, it was intrusive. What had I been thinking?

He hadn't seemed frightened, there was no fear in his expression. There was a grimace as if he felt sudden and severe nausea.

Other than his expression, I could admit now that he really had been a pleasant-looking man.

Just goes to show appearances can be deceiving. It also doesn't speak well of my own judgement.

The patio was next and I divided those pictures even further into two stacks. One pile of pictures of the table, the other pile were pictures all around the table and patio.

It was a Spanish newspaper – La Diaria de Tijuana. I know a little Spanish, it was just daily news and nothing I could see of earth-shaking importance. There was a crossword puzzle about half completed – in Spanish. That was impressive!

The coffee was a to-go cup from the coffee shop in Beverly Hills that we all went to (when we weren't worried about carbs or calories) (or money) and said AJ.

The shop had awesome lattes named after candy bars for obvious reasons. I liked the Snickers and the Reeses. He apparently favored the Almond Joy. That fit with the faint smell of chocolate, almond and coconut.

A small bowl with a floral motif still had a little butter still clinging to the edge of the rim. As soon as I saw it in the picture, I raised my eyes to the small brown sack on my table that I hadn't really registered until then. Muriel had left her muffin-of-hope sitting by my tissue box when she was crying earlier.

Too bad I was on my diet.

It would be character building to see how long I could ignore it.

Easier if I stuck it in the drawer in the bottom of the refrigerator, so I did.

There was another stack of pictures for the left interior of his trailer (left of the door). It turned out to be the kitchen area. Then there was a stack for the right side, the living area, of the trailer. I hadn't gotten much of the bedroom area, just through door with the curtain open. The same with the bathroom area.

He got brownie points for his housekeeping.

He had apparently conquered the place-for-everything-and-everything-in-its-place goal. Dishes that matched the bowl on the table were draining in the small sink. There was mail in a holder attached to the side of the cabinet, cleverly made large enough to accommodate both a variety of flat and some small padded envelopes. A book of stamps was thumb-tacked beside it.

The television had DVDs neatly stacked underneath it. There were no cans or bottles stacked around.

I have an excuse, pet food takes up a

lot of storage space.

Just for the record.

There were some medicine bottles along the back of the bathroom sink. That was normal, he was about my age, after all.

His bed was made.

My animals sleep in mine even after I get up, or mine would be too.

Just saying…

I got up and stood in my doorway and looked over. What had I missed?

With Buddy on his leash, I wandered over, pensively. Sixteen steps.

I continued down the hard road to the east of us, all the way to the dead end and back. It was a good half-mile and I lost track of steps because Buddy had me weaving back and forth to track turtles, opossums, grasshoppers.

I neither saw nor thought of anything

of interest. Pretty walk, not interesting. As I neared home I saw Pete in his ubiquitous cart talking to Nathan.

As I drew near they stopped talking.

Not being good at social cues, I hesitated long enough to wonder why.

Then it dawned on me that I hadn't exactly endeared myself to either of them. I took a deep breath. Turning over a new leaf and all that.

"I have some brownies if you guys are interested." I smiled and hoped I didn't look like the Cheshire Cat. At least I had my teeth in, all of them!

Nathan brightened up and I retrieved a couple for them on paper towels.

"Have you heard anything more about Mr. Cross?" I aimed the question at anyone who would answer.

"We were just talking about it. I know

a guy at the SO who said it was poison." Pete volunteered. Cynically, I figured he answered because he felt he owed me for calling him.

Pete knew or was related to everyone in the county; I had discovered that my first day here. Also learned that he was a retired fireman, had three adult children, two of them living with him here at the park.

"What kind of poison?"

"I don't know that; but it can't be anything I have. Other than a little glyphosate on the rock roads, I don't keep any poisons around." He lit a cigarette. "Well, there's ant poison." He took a deep drag. "I also have wasp spray."

Nathan chimed in. "Things like coolant can be poison, too."

"Thanks." Pete answered wryly. "I needed something else to worry about." He flicked an ash. "The door to my shed is usually locked, you know. Well, sometimes it's locked." Another drag. "Besides, old Albert and I got along pretty good." He looked sideways at Nathan. "If anyone didn't, it was you. You found him, didn't you?"

"I called 911, too. Why would I do that if I killed him? Besides, why would you kill someone over dog poop?" Nathan gave a petulant and unnecessary tug on his dog's leash.

Definitely hit a nerve, there.

"I also heard he had a lot of money. Nathan offered that tidbit to deflect the attention from himself. Whether it was true or not, it changed the focus of the conversation. "He paid his rent a year at a time." He glanced at Pete to test the veracity of that rumor.

"Wouldn't be surprised if he kept it under his mattress or in his refrigerator behind his endless supply of beer."

"Didn't he call a deputy on you, the other night?" Pete asked me, adroitly changing suspects and subjects at the same time. "How did you feel about that?"

I took a step back. I hadn't expected that. I could be a suspect. To hear it from someone who had been friendly to me took me aback. Of course, I hadn't been very friendly back.

New leaf, new leaf. I chanted to myself. "I was irritated. I had yelled at him earlier because he had scared me the night before. I guess we were even. The deputy was a nice kid, by the way."

"One of my cousin's boys." Pete commented.

"Probably arsenic." Opined Nathan. "It's in practically everything. "

"Like what?" Pete was skeptical.

"Fruits, seeds, that sort of stuff; the pressure treated wood you used to build his porch." Nathan looked down at the slats and shifted his weight; he'd been standing quite a while. "You built my porch, too. Could have been you, you know. Everybody knows you favor that Muriel woman and she preferred Albert."

Pete's complexion turned the color of the nearby hibiscus flowers. I'll probably never know if it was rage at Nathan for the insinuations (both of them) or embarrassment at the truth, because I decided I had been there long enough.

"See you, guys." I turned and headed back. It was time to treat Patches again. Her pretty face looked at me so trustingly as she came out and let me do my worst. This round was so much stronger than the last round of drugs that the receptionist at the vet had double-checked the order with the computer twice and then gone back to double-check with the doctor. I took a minute to stroke Patches' pretty white fur and murmur reassurances, but we both knew what was coming and I decided that putting it off was scaring her more. Hopefully the day would come soon that I could just sit and love her, and she could just lay in my lap and purr.

Poison, huh. I mentally listed the people who, ostensibly, had a motive. Nathan, either one or both of the Jaxsons, me, Pete (apparently). The daughter, maybe; was he really one of those uber-wealthy guys living in a trailer out of some kind of perversity? Was there insurance?

Who else? I decided to go visit Muriel. She knew him better than anyone.

CHAPTER 7

NEW POINT OF VIEW

Problem. I didn't know which home was hers.

I started to turn back and ask Pete, but fortunately stopped just in time. That would be appearing to rub it in that he had been sweet on her.

I was learning tact!

So, instead, Buddy and I wandered up and down the roads until I saw someone on their porch and asked where Muriel lived.

"She's in that awful pink trailer. Nice woman, no taste at all," the squat cat-lady answered. She didn't look like a cat, more like a mouse. She had very short, straight gray hair, prominent ears, buck-dentures, and beady eyes. Please take notice I refrained from the more perceptually derogatory "rat." I should get points for second guessing my critical nature. I called her cat-lady because there had to be at least twelve of them inside her screened porch. If she died in her sleep there wouldn't be anything left by morning.

I love cats, don't get me wrong. I have two. However, I am not blind to their natures.

"I'm Carlotta, by the way." She wiped some unknown substance off her hand onto her housecoat and held it out to shake hands with me.

That's not going to happen. I shifted hands on the leash to make shaking impractical if not impossible. "I'm Patty. It's nice to meet you."

I back-tracked to the pink mobile home. The color wasn't so bad. I kind of liked it. Maybe not quite so much of it, though. Especially when her neighbors were all shades of white.

Cat-lady didn't have much room to talk, hers was chartreuse.

We knocked on the carport door because the path to the front door was overgrown with – whatever it was - growing on either side of it. She pushed open the door. She had apparently refreshed her make-up and ruined it again. "Come in. The detective just left." She turned and went back in, expecting me to follow.

"I have Buddy with me, I don't want to tie him outside. I just wanted to check in on you."

"He can come in." Her voice trailed back from the dark, cool interior.

All windows were all covered, a big contrast to my own habitat. The furniture suited her, it was feminine and kind of gave the impression of dainty. Probably because there was even more pink involved in her interior decorating. There were different kinds of needlework everywhere, cross-stitch, plastic canvas needlepoint coasters, knit afghans and a crocheted shawl hanging on a kitchen chair. When this was over maybe we could be friends!

"What beautiful work! All yours?" I complimented her sincerely.

"Yes, yes. I get bored easily." She settled into what was obviously her chair of choice. There were knitting needles, a mug with pens and crochet hooks, needle-nose pliers and a sewing basket all within easy reach. There was even an open tackle box open on a shelf under the lamp table. The chains and wire glittered among beads and stones. "Crafts can be so expensive. I used to sell them but you can't really make enough money to do anything except buy more supplies to keep making things."

"Then, one day it seems, everyone you know has everything they want that you know how to do and you're stuck with looking for another avenue of cash."

A definite truism. I knew that for a fact.

I settled on one end of the sofa and my dog immediately gathered himself to jump up next to me. There wasn't room in my trailer to sit with him unless it was in bed, and he wanted to take advantage of the couch.

"No, Big Dog." I said softly and put my foot on his leash, close to his collar; holding his head and neck close to the ground so he had to settle for the rug.

"You look a little better." I lied.

See, tact!

"That's a very pretty necklace." That part was true. Enameled flowers featured in her jewelry today.

"I guess I'm getting over the shock. Have you lost a husband or boyfriend?"

"Yes, two husbands. They were very ill, however; they weren't killed."

She pinkened. She must have felt she had brought up something painful to me. More time had elapsed for me, however. While the hurt never goes away, it does get remote with time.

"He was too." She said it very quietly.

I must have looked surprised. Hopefully I looked surprised and not skeptical. He had certainly looked healthy and fit.

"A tumor. No one else knew. It was one reason we hadn't gotten married." She blinked away a tear. "It was very like my late Carroll's."

Probably insurance issues. Insurance and income were the most common impediments to senior companionship. I wondered, however if her pronouncement was just wishful explanation. In this day and age they could have just lived together and no one would have thought twice about it.

"My late husband died of cancer as well." She continued.

My brain had to shift gears quickly. "Carroll?"

I had forgotten she had told me her husband had died of cancer. Her eyes started to fill with tears again.

"Can I get you a glass of water or something?" I asked just as she buried her face in her hands.

"Please." I know it was more to get me to leave the room than a desire for water, but I got to my feet and headed to where I had seen a door to the kitchen. Buddy popped to his feet and lumbered after me.

He settled a little away from me as I tried to quietly open cabinet doors, looking for a glass. Silly to try to be quiet, I suppose. It made me feel like I was surreptitiously looking for something. Just to the right of the sink – where there should have been glasses – I found plates and bowls. To the left of the sink, where there should have been plates and bowls, I found a small pharmacy. There were bottles and bottles of allergy medication, vitamins, pain killers, and more serious stuff on the upper shelves. Things I couldn't pronounce, both prescription and non-prescription, but all unpronounceable.

It's a good thing I was out of sight, I was so surprised I just looked for a minute. Then I shut the door, tried another random cabinet and finally found the glasses.

Her refrigerator had one of those water-in-the-door-things that irritate me because they never seem to aim the water the same place I put the glass. They also randomly spit out ice on the floor. Stupid appliance. I braved it anyway and cleaned up the mess with a paper towel. I tossed it into an open trash can by the door.

She had collected herself a bit when we (yes, Buddy upped and followed me) came back. He eyed the couch and caught my look.

Then he huffed and laid back down on the rug.

I handed her the glass and sat back down.

"Did the detective say anything? All I've heard are unsubstantiated rumors and hate to credit any of them; you are a much more credible source." Oops, that sounded a little cold blooded.

She shook her head and put the glass down on a coaster with a pink flower design. Apparently she didn't think twice about my choice of words. Maybe she was mollified that I would consider her the ultimate on information about him.

"No. They wouldn't tell me anything. However, they called his daughter and she called me. I'm not sure how she got my number; don't really care." She shook her head. "She was very upset. More, I think, embarrassed at their lack of a relationship than concerned that he had died. She did say they told her it was most likely either murder or suicide. Poison."

"Did you tell the detective he was sick?"

She pinkened again. I was never going to play cards with this woman…against her, maybe…but not as a partner.

"No. He was so determined that no one know that it didn't feel right to tell a stranger." She shifted and drank a little more water. "I'm not sure why I told you, except maybe because you understand what I am going through and what he was starting to go through. He was afraid of the long illness, not of dying. We had talked about it a lot. He was afraid of being helpless. He hated going to doctors."

"They will figure it out on their own."

Picking at the bracelet on her wrist, she was almost pointedly not looking me in the eye. "Anyone who has seen someone they love go out that way would rather take almost any other option. We had talked about all of his choices." She picked up her glass again and looked like she was going to say something else. She put the glass down again and missed centering it on the coaster. As soon as she let go and started to speak it tipped and poured water and ice into her knitting bag.

" Shoot!" She jumped up and grabbed the glass. Then she picked up the bag and headed for the kitchen.

It was a good break in the conversation. Most conversations drag on interminably in my opinion. This one had been long enough.

"I'm sorry. What a mess! Buddy and I'll just go now. Stop by my place anytime."

We made it out the door before she could stop us.

The park's community shower/laundry room was just across the way through a gate. I decided to use the lavatory there, it would get us out of sight faster and, besides that, I was old, I needed to use it.

Someone had put the toilet paper roll on backward. Everyone knows it should hang on the side away from the wall.

I changed it.

CHAPTER 8

NEW MOTIVES

It was later in the day that I decided to examine every corner of my recently acquired travel trailer. The thought of an undiscovered stash of cash such as Albert may have left in his, made the search a clear choice against boredom.

An hour later (like I have mentioned several times, it is only ten steps from bedroom to bathroom) I was forced to admit a lack of largess from a previous owner. Did Albert really have money? Did he, indeed, hide it rather than invest it? Somehow he seemed smarter than that. There was the foreign language thing, for example. Who knows, maybe his parents spoke Spanish and he grew up with it. It seemed more likely, however that he was both well-educated and well-traveled.

Sweaty and dirty, I settled at my table to consider the thought of poison again. It was rather a drastic way to rid an old man of hidden money. Plus, he had already gone to the coffee shop and was reading his paper out-of-doors, pointing out probable daylight. Being daylight, when would they have a chance to search his trailer without being seen?

I wondered about the daughter. Would she show up here or have the body shipped to her? Surely the latter would be more convenient. It's a good thing I'm learning to keep such thoughts to myself, they sounded ghoulish even to me.

Still, insurance? Stocks? Was there consideration given to Muriel? She hadn't sounded affluent, or even comfortable. Had they been as close as Muriel thought they had been?

Illness also gave rise to the question of suicide. My mind and fingers went immediately back to the picture of the newspaper. NOBODY would kill themselves on purpose in the middle of a crossword puzzle.

The photos were once again spread out before me as I nibbled on a peanut butter and honey sandwich (jelly having been devoured in one sitting last week to remove it from the refrigerator and temptation). Honey was good for you, everyone said so.

The pictures of the bathroom sink were on top of the next stack. There was Calcium, B17, Advil, Tylenol. A couple of aerosol cans included anti-perspirant and shave cream.

Speaking of drugs, it was time to dose Patches again. Once again she tolerated my ministrations and hid herself when I let go of her. The rash wasn't getting any better.

It had to be a trick of the light that I saw movement in Albert's trailer later that evening, when I took Buddy out for his late evening walk. Just because no one would rob Albert in daylight didn't mean they wouldn't creep into our quiet cul-de-sac and rob him after he died.

Outrage swept over me at this intrusion; discounting entirely that I had also intruded. My trespass had at least been well intentioned. Solving the mystery of his death would be a service to him, and to Muriel and the daughter (what was her name? Effie? No wonder she didn't speak to him. Really. Effie?) If solving the mystery also provided me with a best-seller, so much the better.

One of the neighbor dogs apparently agreed with me, he was raising an infernal racket across the way.

Like many of my worst decisions, I didn't stop to think about this one either. I stepped up on the patio and pounded self-righteously on the door with the flat of my hand. "Open up, no one should be in there!" I stepped back to see if I could see through the window frosting. As an afterthought, "I've already called the police!"

There was no sound from inside. I thought I saw a flicker of dark moving across the room. Abruptly I was certain I was not alone on the patio. I turned slowly and was sure Albert was standing on the end of the patio.

The woman from the mobile home that backed up to our spaces banged open her back door and yelled at her yappy little terrier to shut up. The dog was then rewarded with entry and the lighted rectangle disappeared. So did Albert, if I really had seen him.

CHAPTER 9

NEW INSIGHT

"Good morning, Ms. Decker."

I turned down the music I was listening to as I stared at the computer screen and pondered the practicality of being a novelist. Then I used my tongue to see if my teeth were in. Fortunately they were.

"Why so formal? I was Patty last time we talked." It was Pete at the door, on two feet and at least twenty feet from his golf cart.

"I thought you might be mad at me after I threw you under the bus the other day when we were talking to Nathan."

It took me a minute to figure out what he was talking about. "Oh, the deputy thing, forget it. We were all a little distraught and throwing out different scenarios was normal. I had as good a motive as either of you did. None of them particularly good motives."

"Thanks for that." He was craning his neck to look up at me.

I checked to see where the cats were and moved the dog door to step out and down. "What's up? Did the Sheriff's office decide what happened to Albert?"

"Not entirely. I gather the poison was Cyanide, but that's all I know. Funny, poison is why I'm here. Albert had sugar ants in his trailer. The little buggers had actually gotten into a closed jar of peanut butter, if you can believe that! I asked Nathan if he had them and he does, too."

"If you have them, I'll just treat the whole cul-de-sac. I'm just using borax and sugar at the moment."

"Are they those teeny-tiny ants that I keep dumping out of my animals dry-food bowls in the mornings?"

"Most likely."

"Borax and sugar don't sound very dangerous. It won't hurt me or the animals? Do I need to take them away for a while or something?"

"No. It won't hurt you. If it doesn't work, I'll have to use an insecticide. Then I'll just treat the ground under the trailers."

When I got back to the computer I pulled up the internet and typed in ant killer. Borax and sugar figured prominently.

The next most popular was arsenic

based but I had to follow several strings to find that out. At least I called them strings... Paths? What the heck do you call it when you jump from search to search to find out something? Does it matter? Was I wasting brain cells thinking about it?

I typed in Cyanide and ant killers. Clear back in the 1800s the Californians used cyanide to kill ants but that went by the wayside when other products did it better and more safely. Typical of California, everything used to be legal there and now everything is restricted.

I had a creepy sensation on the back of my neck like I wasn't alone.

I just started following cyanide to see what was what. Used in photography, it was part of a developing medium. Who did I know was a photographer?

"Patty! Are you coming to Bingo

tonight?" A strange woman was standing outside my door. My first reaction was to slam the door. I was busy, damn it.

I actually smiled, though it may have been more of a grimace. "I hadn't thought about it. I'm sorry, I don't remember your name." Vaguely I recognized her as maybe the woman who sold the cards and markers.

"Sorry. I'm Sally. We were hoping you would come back." She backed up a little and I suddenly understood I was supposed to get up and come out there just because she wanted me to.

I wanted friends, yes; but I wanted them on my terms. I only wanted to see people when I *wanted* to see people.

With what I hoped was not an audible sigh (see, I am learning) I levered my body out of the comfortable dent in my bench cushion and emerged like a moth from my cocoon.

"I guess I didn't realize it was tonight. What kind of snack should I bring? Is there a schedule or a protocol there?"

She looked like the quintessential organizer. She wore a sundress and pearls, her shoes matched her dress. There was undoubtedly hairspray involved in her hairstyle.

"Not really. Whatever you like. We do have a couple of people with dietary restrictions. Honestly most of us don't pay much attention, if they need special stuff, they can bring it. I do try to accommodate with sugar free things every so often for the gluten people and diabetics."

It sounded like she added that last so that she didn't sound completely intolerant. "Sugar free is probably popular." I offered on behalf of the diabetic contingent. I refrained from giving an impromptu lecture on just what was gluten-free.

She nodded. I got the impression she wasn't done with her errand. I decided to speed this up a little rather than invite her to sit down and sip sweet tea (which I abhorred and didn't have anyway). "I don't think I'm going to make it this evening. I'll come next time, though, and bring something." I half turned to move the dog/cat-gate and get back to my research.

"We kind of hoped Muriel would come, too. Have you seen her? She's not answering her door or her phone and, well, we know you saw her yesterday. How's she doing?"

The thought struck me that this was one of the "friends" who did not tell her that her boyfriend was dead.

I wouldn't answer her knock, either.

It took me a minute to come up with a

suitably innocuous answer. "I'm sure I don't know. I would think, however, that bingo is pretty far down on her list of priorities right now."

"Do you know what happened to Albert?"

I suppose I had opened up the subject, albeit obliquely; so it was acceptable now for her to ask.

"The deputies are investigating several residents of the park to determine which one of us killed him." I heard a little gasp but had already turned my back on her. Sally was no longer on my list of potential friends. It's interesting that under other circumstances it may have taken me months to figure out her true character under southern manners. I did shut the door this time.

I brooded for a little bit, petting my animals and reveling in the unconditional love they offered without pretense.

I shut the computer off and popped a DVD into the television. I needed to get away from murder for at least the evening. Ice Age was a good choice.

Mary Lu Scholl

CHAPTER 10

NEW GHOST

Patches let out a pathetic meow when I put the ointment on her back and suddenly I couldn't take it anymore. I hugged her gently and put her in the carrier that was doing double-duty as a step into the bed. She collapsed on the fleece lining the bottom. I dressed and looked at the clock. If we were too early, I would just hold her and wait.

The girls at the desk were experienced enough to just take one look at my face and show us into a room. The veterinarian and his technician came in together.

"If you can't look at her and tell me she's improving; I can't do this to her anymore."

I pulled her gently out of the crate and she made like a pathetic little white puddle with patches of brown and gray. The doctor gently touched her back where the skin was bubbled and raw.

I could see the answer in his face. He looked at me and all I could do was nod.

"Now?"

I nodded and took her back. Words were out of the question. He disappeared. The technician slipped out and then back in. She had questions, cremation? I nodded. Do I want to pay for it now? I nodded and dug out my credit card without putting Patches down. The doctor came back and asked if I had done this before.

Again mutely, I nodded.

"Do you want to hold her?" I looked at him, incredulity battling with tears. Of course I would hold her. I nodded again.

"It's very quick. Are you ready?"

I nodded again. It was quick. One last kiss on her head and I surrendered her to the technician, smiled weakly at the Veterinarian and tears spilled over.

The crate was light without her weight and I had to resist throwing it in a fit of temper when I got back to my truck. Why Patches? She was so sweet and so young, only three. What had I done wrong? I had tried so hard all summer to make her better.

I found my way home and made it into the trailer to my remaining animals. I gathered them close and fell asleep for a good part of the day.

The phone woke me up. It was my

son, undoubtedly just checking in. I couldn't face talking to him. I texted him and told him I couldn't talk, but was everything okay?

He texted back with the message that everything was fine, he would call me again the next day or so.

I looked at the screen and realized I had another text, this one from Muriel.

What are you doing? Do you want to come over for tea or something?

It had been about an hour ago. I texted back. *Sorry, I had to put one of my cats to sleep this morning and have been indisposed. I wasn't ignoring you; I was asleep and didn't see your message until just now. I'll see you tomorrow.*

Her response was prompt. *I understand completely. Sometimes you just have to step in and do what is best, no matter how hard it may be.*

I ate a comfort-dinner of home-made macaroni and cheese, tomatoes topped with my guacamole.

With a sigh I opened up my computer and typed Cyanide into the search engine again. I didn't have to solve this mystery in order to write a book. I could make it end anyway I wanted to, but I did have to know more about cyanide if I was going to incorporate it.

I heard a low growl and glanced down at Buddy. The fur on his neck was standing up and I followed his eyes to the bench across the table from me.

Albert was there. He put up his hands in a conciliatory or even pleading posture but it was too late, I screamed. He disappeared.

Buddy and I stared at where he had been. Why would he haunt me? Late husbands I could understand. An animus neighbor?

Buddy and I left the trailer for a long walk. By the time we made it back I had accepted that I had to understand why he appeared. There must be a reason. Maybe because I was working on the case (sort of) or maybe just because I was the closest person physically to his place of death.

We stopped at his patio and I sat down on one of the PVC chairs. Buddy didn't like the wood floor. Maybe it was the slats, or maybe he could smell the arsenic Nathan had claimed was part of the treated wood.

"I don't know if you're listening, but I'm sorry I screamed. You scared the crap out of me." I let the apology hang out there in the twilight.

"I am not normally afraid of ghosts, but frankly, you were completely unexpected. We weren't even friends. I am trying to find out what happened to you. If that is what you want, rest assured I'm trying." I hesitated and watched as lightning bugs winked on around me (us). "If you want me to help, you could probably clear up a few things for me."

"The ghosts I knew before never tried to talk to me, that I know of, anyway; but I have read it is possible."

"I suppose it takes practice. I just want to assure you I won't scream again; or, at least, I'll try not to."

Buddy and I went home and put an end to a long, rotten, miserable day. Ashes curled up under my chin and her purring calmed me down. Tomorrow was time enough for whatever would happen next.

CHAPTER 11

NEW SUSPECTS

I woke up and slid out of bed, heading for the bathroom when I slipped my glasses on and saw Albert sitting at the table again. I started to scream again and saw by his expression that he knew it. I clamped a hand over my mouth.

"Out." I instructed. "Out, out, out. Give me an hour."

I fumed all through morning ablutions. I even put in my teeth after a breakfast of oatmeal. Ashes was crunching kibble and Buddy was chewing his dental bone when

Albert came back. His expression was tentative.

"Ground rules. I don't receive company until I am dressed. YOU are company. I will, however, get dressed as soon as I get up, and will open the door so you can tell."

Albert nodded.

"Have you figured out how to talk to me?"

He shook his head.

"Do you know how you died?"

He nodded.

"It was poison, cyanide."

He nodded his head again, but it seemed to indicate acceptance rather than agreement.

"Do you know how it happened?"

He shook his head.

"I'm going to look at cyanide again on

the internet; I keep getting interrupted. Then I'm going to talk to Pete again and see if he knows anymore. Maybe Nathan, too. He seems to always know what's going on."

"Muriel is pretty upset, by the way."

He nodded and disappeared.

I pulled up cyanide again. After photography it brought up fishing. Fishing with cyanide? Who knew? A little further reading discounted that as having any pertinence here. It was for catching live fish in a reef environment in the Far East, mostly.

Next it brought up mining, making paper and making plastic. It explained that most cases of cyanosis are work-related industrial accidents. A substantial percentage due to fires, with firefighters top on the list with toxic smoke inhalation from burning plastics. Didn't Nathan used to be a firefighter? It seems like I heard that somewhere. Maybe it was Pete. He would know the chemical reactions, then, that would be toxic. He also had access to all sorts of chemicals as maintenance and landscape manager for the park.

I was getting square eyes from staring at the screen. I skimmed the articles about mining and releasing gold from ore. At the end of that article it cross-referenced to Jewelry making and cleaning. I thought about that as I hit the back arrow to get back to my original list of uses. It continued on, but I needed to think about that jewelry reference.

Muriel. She made jewelry. I remembered the tackle box and the needle-nosed pliers. Then I remembered our conversation about the cancer and long, slow illnesses. She had already watched someone she loved go out that way and was facing it again if she was to be believed.

I had just put Patches to sleep yesterday. She had started to tell me something that day at her house. What had she texted me last night? I looked it up. She said she understood and that sometimes we had to do what was right.

Surely she wouldn't apply that to an adult human who could make his own choices.

How would she give it to him? Did he take it willingly? No, I already discounted that – the crossword puzzle thing.

I stepped out on the porch and called softly, "Albert?"

He appeared quickly and quietly. It seemed like he was marginally more substantial this time.

"Had you talked about suicide with Muriel? She may seem to think it is a reasonable response to a long cancer battle."

He nodded.

"What did you think?"

"No."

It was a faint but definite answer. "I'm not sure she respected your wishes. She may have been focused on the effects of your illness on herself." Albert winked out.

Nathan came around the corner with his lab, Angie. "Who were you talking to?" He looked around curiously. "I thought maybe Pete was over here."

"No. I was talking to Albert; trying to figure this thing out."

"If he answers, let me know. I've always wanted to meet a ghost."

I just smiled at him. He must have considered that an invitation. He sat down.

That was okay. I needed a sounding board. "How well do you know Pete?"

"Just from here at the park. We've

shared a few beers and every so often we get on each other's nerves and don't talk for a month or so."

"Disagreements about Muriel?"

Nathan looked startled. "No. Why would you ask that?"

"I don't know." I hedged. "She's attractive. You mentioned that Pete was enamored of her; and so was Albert. Were there others who may have been more serious than she thought?"

Albert suddenly appeared on the other end of the glider I was sitting on. Since Nathan didn't say anything or get up and run, I had to assume he couldn't see him.

Nathan thought about it and pet Angie's ears. "I guess you're thinking someone was jealous of Muriel enough to kill his competition." He was thoughtful. "She wasn't my type. Maybe it's just been too soon since I lost my wife." A little more thought. "There are a number of single men here. More men than some places, but also a lot of the men are married. There was one, a caretaker for the house across the road. The lady who owns it keeps it rented out but it seems to be empty a lot and he's over there fixing and mowing all the time. Jesus?" Nathan gave it the Mexican pronunciation. "Muriel is a nice woman. I've seen her give him a muffin and a coke once in a while when it's hot." He shook his head, though. "I can't see it. He and Pete are friends, too. Since he's also in maintenance and landscaping they have a lot in common."

So they have a lot of the same knowledge...

"Pete had it pretty bad for Muriel for a while. He was just too busy for her, though. Some women are pretty high maintenance as far as attention goes. Between kids, his job and his ex-wife…" Nathan looked up at me. "You did know he bought his ex a mobile home and moved her here when her last husband died and left her homeless? Pete's a nice guy. Albert had more time for her."

I was distracted, with one eye on Albert as we both listened to Nathan. I had asked Nathan for his opinion because he seemed to know everything about everybody, This was the longest single speech he had made. Albert blushed at Nathan's last statement. I didn't know ghosts could blush.

I had heard enough and needed to think. It was time for Nathan to leave, I had what I wanted.

New leaf, new leaf. I remembered my manners and offered him a pop or some water but fortunately he turned me down.

"Angie and I have to finish her walk.

See you later."

Albert was also gone when I turned around.

I wondered briefly why it was so much easier to get to know the men around here than the women. I'd only really interacted with Muriel, Sally, and briefly, the cat lady and the bird woman.

CHAPTER 12

NEW EXCUSES

Albert popped in again just as I was fixing my dinner and feeding both animals.

I nearly jumped out of my skin. I started to yell at him, but stopped myself. He couldn't exactly knock or tap me on the shoulder, could he? I was dressed, and I hadn't given any afternoon or evening restrictions. Most people don't eat dinner and go to bed at eight-thirty.

It was getting dark out and the shadeless, plug-in table lamp I had bought to battle my winking lights gave him a kind of shimmering quality. Taking a deep breath, I smiled wanly. "What brings you here?"

He waved his hand toward himself and then at the door. His movements were jerky and his face contorted with some sort of emotion.

Buddy scratched at the door – he was faster at interpretation than I was. We both left by conventional means, Albert was already on his patio waiting for us. There was a light on inside the trailer. The police tape was still there. I had abided by it and by damn, whoever was in there should have to as well! I knocked loudly on the door while I dialed the Sheriff's Office.

Why is it I know the SO number off the top of my head?

The light went out and all was still.

Gimme a break! If I saw the light and knocked on the door do you think you're going to convince me you're gone by turning out the light? It's not like there's a back door.

"This is Patty Decker at the mobile home park where Albert Cross was murdered a few days ago. There is someone in his trailer right now."

"Of course I knocked on the door. How else was I going to find out who's in there?"

"I just live next door. Yes, I can see from my yard."

"You don't have to be rude about it; I'll go home and watch."

Albert wanted me to open his door. He kept popping in and out of his trailer.

"You heard me, they told me to stay out and go home." I said in a loud voice, aimed at the intruder as well as Albert. "I can tell when I'm not wanted." I turned and stepped back to the rip-rap road. Albert popped over right in front of me.

In a low voice I hissed at him. "There's a deputy turning into the park right now, he was just up the road when I called. I'm supposed to pretend I'm leaving to see if they come out before he gets here." His expression was sad.

Realization dawned on me. "Hey, do you know who it is?" He nodded and winked out again.

Lights off, a cruiser pulled up just as I made it back to my grass and turned around.

"Open up. I know you're in there and will shoot the lock off if I have to in order to get in." It was my kid deputy, looking more grown up with his stern expression and the weapon he had drawn.

The door started to open slowly.

Nathan and Angie showed up just as Muriel stepped out. "Hands up." Warned the deputy. "Come out slowly." He turned her against the side of the trailer and efficiently made sure she had no weapons.

"Who are you and what were you doing in there?" He asked her when he was sure she was harmless.

"I have a key. Albert gave me one in case of emergency."

"And what emergency prompted you to cross the police tape and go into an active crime scene where someone was killed? Miss…?"

"I'm Muriel. He was my fiancé. I thought I had left something here and wanted to get it before his daughter shows up." Nathan looked at me and I looked both at him and past him to where Albert stood with his mouth open. I could see him mouth silently – fiancé?

"What? Exactly?"

She hesitated and I could clearly see she didn't have this well-planned out. "Dishes. I bring food over and I wanted to get my dishes back."

"Show me which ones are yours and I will make sure you get them back when this is settled."

"I didn't actually find any of them." She looked over in our direction. "There was a sweater, too." She was getting her story down and her confidence was coming back. "The other deputies must have taken it, and probably the dishes as well." She stood her ground defiantly. "Ask them." She pointed at Nathan and me. "They know me and know I have a right to be here."

Nathan promptly pulled Angie's leash and disappeared around the end of the fence.

Albert was shaking his head slowly from side to side.

"Why didn't you come out when I knocked if you're not up to something? Are you looking for the fortune supposedly hidden under his mattress?" I had to get my two cents in. World's shortest friendship, here.

Deputy Johnson interjected before she could answer. "Let's go to the office and discuss whatever answer you're thinking about giving Miss Patty. Who knows? Maybe I'll show you the dishes and clothing we collected and see if it matches the description you provide me with before we get there."

More gently than I would have expected he led her down the step to the back door of his cruiser. She meekly got in. She looked at me in confusion that melted into a glare. They left after he re-locked Albert's door and pocketed her key.

Albert still stood there as it started to rain on us. "I've been meaning to ask, do you really have a fortune hidden in your trailer – it is a prevailing rumor around here at the moment."

"No." It was a little stronger than the last time he spoke. It held a bit of laughter in it.

"Can you say anything else?" I teased.

He grinned at me and slowly formed another word. "Yes." Then he laughed soundlessly. "Short words."

"Like "I do"? I got the impression you were surprised to find yourself engaged." He gave a snort and shook his head.

"I think I'm sorry we got off on the wrong foot – yes – I know it was my fault." That was as close to an apology as he was going to get, but I had to admit we probably would have been friends.

"Not too late." He winked away.

"Are you okay?" Nathan came back around the fence. "Were you talking to yourself again?"

"They took her away. I wonder if they know she makes jewelry." I turned.

He had no idea what I was talking about, he must have thought I was completely nuts.

Mary Lu Scholl

CHAPTER 13

NEW WAY TO LOOK AT IT

When I woke up it occurred to me that I should share some of my observations with the Sheriff's Office.

It was after ten when I got a call back. "Can you come out and talk to me again? I think I have some things you need to know."

I settled on the patio with my laptop and waited for Deputy Boatright.

Pete showed up first and was perched on his cart talking at me when the Deputy showed up and drew his attention. "Hey Danny. How's my favorite niece?"

Deputy Boatright nodded at me first, then sat in one of the folding chairs I had set out. He shook his leonine head at Pete. "Mandy's going to a dance Saturday; can you believe that?"

"She's only twelve! What can you be thinking to let her go?"

"Twelve, my eye. She's fourteen going on twenty. It's a school dance."

The guys commiserated a little longer on children growing up and I became reconciled to Pete being part of the conversation. I might even get an answer or two with Pete an apparent relative and at least somewhat in my corner!

"Is Muriel home yet?" I started off.

"Here, I thought you had things to tell me." Deputy Boatright answered.

"Well, some of it depends on whether or not I am right about a few other things. It was cyanide, right?"

The deputy looked at Pete reproachfully.

Pete looked down at his phone, made an excuse and a hasty exit.

"I've been researching cyanide."

"Interesting hobby." He interrupted.

"I'm a writer." I explained, and considered that sufficient. "Cyanide is fascinating. It is used for so many different things, I wanted to make sure you knew that Muriel makes jewelry. It is used in jewelry making."

"I was under the impression that she was enamored of Mr. Cross."

"Yes, but did you know her late

husband died of a long, slow cancer?"

"I believe it was mentioned once or twice. I got the impression it was a sympathy ploy." He grimaced.

"You do know that Mr. Cross also had a tumor."

He looked at me sharply. He apparently had not shared that with my presumed source, Pete. "I don't know how you knew that. I was under the impression your own relationship with the deceased was somewhat acrimonious. Very unlikely, then, that he would have shared that with you and not with his daughter or fiancé."

Then he made that scenario worse. "The friendlier relationship with you could strengthen the possibility that you killed him out of jealousy when he proposed to another woman." His whole body went on alert as he scrutinized me to see what my response to that would be. "How did you feel about him wanting to marry another woman?"

THAT hadn't even occurred to me. "Muriel knows." I threw her under the bus. "She told me. Albert, Mr. Cross, didn't like me at all and it was mutual. Besides that I've only been here a very short time and am recently widowed myself. Give me a little time to get over it, please."

"I'm sorry for your loss. Local?"

"No. I moved here to be close to my son."

"So he is close by?"

"No. He moved."

I could tell he had to bite his tongue not to answer that one or enquire farther. He still had more he wanted to know, however. "Just why would his fiancé tell you? You're the one trying to point the finger in her direction." One golden eyebrow raised.

This was not going well at all. "All I'm interested in is solving the mystery for a book I'm writing."

"So, how did you do it in the book?" He raised both eyebrows this time.

"I didn't do it!" I actually sputtered. "I'm new here, and thought that Muriel and I could be friends, until I decided she had euthanized my neighbor."

"Interesting choice of words." He frowned a little at me, but was more interested than confrontational, thank goodness.

"I had to put one of my cats to sleep and Muriel was very sympathetic." I paused.

"Remind me never to be sympathetic around you – I may be accused of an assassination attempt or something."

I made a face at him. "Believe it or not, I'm trying to be pleasant and it's an effort. You might meet me halfway."

"All of her other comments by themselves, taken out of context, were actually pretty innocuous. It wasn't until you put them all together that they sounded damning. Muriel said she was sure that a quick death was better than a lingering death. She had lost her husband to the same cancer her boyfriend was diagnosed with. It just clicked that she may have taken it into her own hands, for his benefit." I added. "Maybe for her own benefit, not wanting to go through that again."

"That's a pretty big stretch." He commented.

With a very rare burst of complete honesty, I met his eyes. "No. It's not."

"Look, had he eaten a muffin with his coffee? Could you tell if the poison was in the muffin or was it in the coffee? Can you tell if it was a tablet or in liquid form? A gas was highly unlikely."

"You don't really expect me to answer any of that, do you?" Now he looked amused.

"I'm not as good at forensics as I sound. Can you tell if two muffins came from the same batch?" I chewed my lip and dislodged my bottom denture, damn it. "Although, if it was added after it was baked, it wouldn't show up in the other muffins." I added, as an afterthought. "Would it help if you had another of her muffins to compare?" I looked him in the eye.

"How would I know if she baked either one or both of them? Yes – by the way – I can pin down a batch match." He asked, somewhat interested.

"Fingerprints? Can you lift them off paper?"

"Show me." His eyes narrowed.

"Don't touch whatever it is, let me get it."

"I've already touched the outside, but nothing on the inside." I gestured for him to go in the trailer ahead of me, since if I went in first he would have to go around me to get Muriel's bag with a muffin out of the fridge. Going around someone in that trailer was, if even possible, way too intimate an act for me and a suspicious deputy detective. I followed him instead. "In the refrigerator, the drawer on the far bottom. She left it here - by accident, I presume – right after Mr. Cross died. She said she was coming over to check and see if it was true. I'm the one who told her to call you, by the way." I looked him in the eye. " You're welcome." I added dryly.

He retrieved it with gloves that materialized out of nowhere.

"Don't leave town." He told me as he hopped up into his big truck and left.

I sort of hoped Muriel wasn't back home. I didn't know how far Muriel was going to go in reaction to my apparent betrayal.

It was very late before I could get to sleep that night.

CHAPTER 14

NEW LOOK AT AN OLD DRUG

Buddy and Ashes both got me up the next morning. He was patting my feet with his paw and she was head-butting me to get me up to feed them. My first instinct was to look for Patches. I cried while I fed the other two.

Then I cried for both late husbands. The day was just going to suck.

I happened to look out the kitchen window and saw Muriel talking to Nathan over by Albert's. Fortunately Buddy had already gone out so I didn't have to leave the trailer and risk running into her.

I turned on Rat Pack Radio on high and shut all the blinds I could reach. Cowardice, yeah. I had to wonder what I said had been passed along to her by way of interrogation. Maybe the detective hadn't even finished checking on things yet, hadn't even talked to her again.

My phone rang in the middle of a DVD I was watching later in the day.

"Ms. Decker?"

Okay. I decided right then that Miss was preferable to either Ma'am or Ms. "Yes?"

"I'm only telling you this so you will leave Muriel Johnson alone. The muffins matched. She volunteered a small container of cyanide she used for jewelry, we didn't even have to get a search warrant, but it was not a match to the contents of Mr. Cross's stomach. It made a pretty good story, so go ahead and put it in your book, but leave this case to us, now." Deputy Boatright admonished me.

I wished I had an old fashioned bake-light landline so I could slam the receiver.

I took Buddy and put him in the truck. His hindquarters just didn't work as well as they used to. Much to his disgust, I had to pick up his furry forty pounds to get him into the truck. We drove until I was calmed down and then we walked.

I was still irked enough to keep walking, but Buddy was starting to drag. His hips were not brand new and between the distance and the heat, he needed to quit.

He needed a haircut. If it was shorter, he would be cooler and happier. While we rested I pulled up dog groomers and made an appointment for the next day, late in the afternoon, but still the next day. That was a surprise. At home I had to make appointments like that at least two weeks in advance.

My phone was slow and I remembered my son had told me to go through every so often and close things using the little box or multiple screen icon thing. I started pushing "x's" and came back to the page listing uses for cyanide.

They had left off that cyanide investigations could ruin reputations. There weren't many more entries.

My eye landed on the very last entry. Cyanide in medicine. Cyanide has been used in the treatment of neoplasms.

Well, that just left me with more questions. I looked up neoplasms and was referenced to malignant tumors.

In a large and bold italic font on the

previous page, readers were advised that the treatment of cancers with cyanide was not approved by the FDA and had, in fact been determined to be so marginally effective as to be simply a matter of opinion; there being no proof of efficacy in any of several referenced studies. It went on that while the treatment under ideal conditions was considered innocuous, the procedures and self-treatment was extremely dangerous due to vagaries in the drug and differences in interpretation of the best way to proceed.

Well, the Federal Drug Administration only governs the United States.

I remembered the Mexican newspaper Albert had been reading, and pulled up a Mexican Pharmacy.

Not only did Mexico approve of this treatment, it openly advertised it – albeit under a brand name, not quite hiding the ingredients of the treatment, but not being open about them, either.

"Fight your cancer with this proven regimen designed to maximize your health and eliminate malignancies. One bottle B17 essential therapy. Amygdalin, 2 bottles in the package. We recommend 3 tablets to jump start therapy. 1 bottle B15. 1 bottle proteolytic enzimes, Univase Forte. 1 bottle Beta Caroteno. Amygdalin is made of all naturally occurring molecules. There are 2 molecules glucose (sugar) one molecule hydrocyanic acid (an anti-neoplastic compound) and one molecule benzaldehyde (an analgesic). A banner clear down along the bottom of the website page points out the FDA disapproves and that the text on the site cannot be considered medical advice.

Even though it was a Mexican pharmacy website, it offered this information in English and was apparently required to post the disclaimer. Why would you, otherwise?

I wondered how many people had used these products in desperation. Did they actually work? Heaven knows I had no all-encompassing faith in the FDA's impartial evaluation of drugs.

I looked up the lethal dose of Amygdalin. A lethal dose of cyanide is 50 to 300 mg, one 500 mg tablet equals 30 mg cyanide. The Amygdalin was sold in 500 mg tablets.

Hadn't I seen advice to jumpstart therapy with more than one tablet? I scanned back through the original page. Sure enough; it recommends a "jump start" with three tablets.

I called Deputy Boatright. "I know where the cyanide came from." I announced without preamble to his voicemail. This is Mrs. Decker. Call me, please."

Buddy and I started the hike back to the truck.

We were about halfway there when my phone rang. "Now what?" Deputy Boatright was dispensing with small talk right along with me.

"Did you know that in other countries cyanide is used to treat neoplasms – malignant tumors? It's not allowed in the United States, but you can buy it on-line. A whole recommended regimen including Amygdalin is only $250 from Mexican pharmacies. Amygdalin is actually a cyanide compound; giving it a brand or trade name or whatever makes it more palatable."

There was silence on the other end of

the phone. "The padded envelopes had bottles of medication, but they had been unopened so we did not bother with analysis. I'll check and see if they match the contents of his stomach. He may have gotten some from another source before ordering these." Now there was the silence of a disconnect.

CHAPTER 15

NEW CLARITY

Buddy and I walked more slowly and finally made it back to the truck.

The information nagged at me. Suicide. Most likely accidental suicide, but suicide none-the-less. I wondered if his daughter could sue the foreign pharmacy. Probably not, there were plenty of disclaimers even on the website. He was certainly not uneducated and at risk for misunderstanding the implications or the warnings…

We trudged back to my own trailer.

Well, I trudged. Buddy lunged at a saucily tail-twitching squirrel. Obligingly I put him on the twenty-five foot lead I had hooked to the camper steps. He catapulted to the end and reached an abrupt stop. He looked at me reproachfully. If I didn't have him tied, he could catch those tree-rats!

I ignored him and thought about Albert. Another source?

I stepped out and looked around for Nathan. It seemed like every time I tried to talk to Albert, he and Angie showed up. Yup. They were sitting on their porch. I went inside. It was getting dark. I tried calling him tentatively from my trailer. How far away could a ghost hear?

He showed up almost instantly. "Do you just hang out waiting for someone to call you? Or is time different for you? Or are you hovering out of sight and only pop in when given an excuse?" I had questions!

The most important one, however, was none of these. As he started to address my rant I held up my hand to stop him. "Later; sorry. Did you know that the drug you ordered from Mexico was cyanide?"

He nodded. Apparently that was a quicker and easier response than trying to speak when I was obviously in a hurry.

"Who told you about it?" That was my next and even more important question.

"Muriel. Said Carroll tried it." It took several seconds to get out the whole sentence, but gave me all I needed to know.

"Impressive!" I gave him credit for the effort he had been putting into communication. "Are you going to disappear when this is settled?"

He shrugged. This was new to him as well, I guessed.

"I need to get another look in Muriel's kitchen pharmacy." I was talking to myself as much as Albert, out loud. "I wonder if she's in tonight?"

Albert disappeared for a few seconds. "Bingo." He grimaced when he popped back.

"Not your game, huh?" I grinned.

"Not my crowd." He answered slowly and grinned back. Then he popped out.

I went outside. It seems that with ghosts no one needed to stand on ceremony or manners. Small talk was at a minimum and no one thinks twice about it. We could learn a thing or two from associating with them more.

I couldn't just pop over to Muriel's house. I never walk around the park alone, so Buddy would have to go with me. He would be camouflage. As we strolled, Buddy in ecstasy that he was getting another walk so soon, I made a plan..

There's a sidewalk along Highway 44 that goes toward Crystal River. We had walked out to the front of the park and taken that route a couple of times. Muriel's home backed up to the wild area behind it and west of the park. If we strolled that direction we could duck into the woods and creep up on her house from the back.

I was gambling that she was one of the majority who never locked their door – especially when still in the park.

The cat-lady saw us and waved. The manager was already gone home, the office locked up. We went out the gate and turned west.

We went a hundred feet or so and started watching for a break in the woods. One thing I hadn't counted on was the dark.

Not true. I wanted it to be dark so

other people couldn't see us easily. I also wanted it not dark so I could see where the heck we were going.

I know. Never satisfied.

When I tugged on Buddy's leash to head into the gloom of kudzu and Spanish moss draped on the ubiquitous oaks he looked at me like I was crazy.

I could see his thoughts. How often had he looked at me like that when the grass was wet, when it was hot, or when there was snow, and I could see him reminding me *I'm a house dog, Mom."*

"Don't be difficult; just come on or we're never going for another walk." I tugged and he put his head down. The collar slid over his head and off.

"Buddy! Stop that!" I hissed as I tried to get it back over his head quickly. It came off, it should go back on! I finally got it over both ears and it was just getting darker. "Come on, Sweetie."

Canine devotion won out and he reluctantly followed me into the trees. We both stepped over creepers and tried to stay out of sight.

The lights were on inside the trailer to the north of her and the shades were open on the window at that end. It made sense. Why close them when there was no one on that side to see in?

I stopped quietly to see if anyone was in there and could see us but Buddy kept going. "Stop." I hissed again and tugged his leash up short.

He looked at me as if to say *make up your mind, Mom*.

They were apparently just wasting

electricity so we crept past and came to the back of her carport. Fortunately it was open, no fence or shed, just a few plants. I went ahead of Buddy and looked to see if anyone was nearby. Crickets and fireflies, no one else.

I turned the knob as quietly as I could and it opened. I couldn't risk pulling it tightly shut. The metal frames on trailer doors don't absorb sound like good old fashioned wood framed ones. So I just hustled Buddy in with me and headed for the kitchen. One more time I had outsmarted myself. It was dark and no one could see me. It was dark and I couldn't see crap. I opened the flashlight app on my phone. I could take a picture with the flashlight illuminating the shelves.

So, no. You can't take a picture that way. It turns the flashlight off when you open the camera. I tried to take the picture anyway

– I had never tried to see if there was an automatic flash.

Yes! However, it was the wrong cabinet. Which one was it she had the pharmacy in? Flashlight back on, I tried another one. All I could remember is that I was looking for a glass and her kitchen was arranged wrong. Just wrong.

I found it and snapped several pictures to make sure I got clear pictures of everything because I didn't have time to look at them right now.

There were voices from the street; we had to get out now! We crept out and I had to leave the door a little bit ajar to avoid noise; hopefully she would think it just hadn't shut good.

While we were inside her home the little light we had before had gone away. There were clouds that obscured any possible moonlight. The neighbor had turned out his light. I aimed for the northwest to both get away and head for the highway. Buddy gamely tried to follow me. I tried to get him to lead. "Come on Good Boy. Show me where to go."

Before long it was painfully obvious that he was not a cat and couldn't see in the dark.

"I should have brought Ashes. Sure, that wouldn't have drawn any attention!" I still had my voice low, but Buddy heard me and I wound up leading again.

I had another thought. I pulled up Google Maps and sure enough a screen opened with a dot showing me where we were and where the road was. It wasn't easy. I twisted an ankle and bit my tongue to keep from calling out.

Once the highway was in sight I turned

off my screen and we once again strolled as if we did this every night. We overshot Muriel's road, though, and continued on to the road to the east of the park before we turned south towards home. There was no one on that road this time of night, skirting the edge of the park away from most of the full-timers.

We hobbled along slowly. Okay, I hobbled along slowly and just for perversity (apparently) Buddy now led and pulled me along. We finally made it to my porch and inside. I had to hold onto the table to pull myself in from the step, my ankle was just over it, done.

As soon as the door clicked shut behind me I flipped on the lights. Albert popped in uninvited but I forgave him as I opened the gallery on my phone.

There they were. The flash worked. There on the top shelf, with other prescription drugs was a bottle of Amygdalin.

Albert was looking over my shoulder. He reached out a finger to the screen and I obligingly zoomed in on the bottle. He said nothing, but looked very sad.

"Maybe she didn't mean to give you a fatal dose. She might have just been following the directions on the website. Maybe she just thought if one or two was good, three were better. Did she even know they were poison?"

He popped out. We may have become friends of a sort, but not close enough to share the hurt he was undoubtedly feeling with the evidence of his friend's guilt in front of him.

I wondered if I would ever see him again, or if this confirmation was all he was looking for.

I would at least want to know if she did

it on purpose or by accident.

I closed my phone. If it was by accident, had she been punished enough?

Next problem. Should I address this tonight or tomorrow morning? I was sure she noticed the door not shut tight when she got back. How could she not?

If Muriel was just helping him, why didn't she just give him the bottle? Why did she stick them into a muffin? Of course, I only had his word for it that he hadn't known they were in the muffin. My theory on overdosing in the middle of a crossword puzzle probably wouldn't carry much weight.

I pulled out the card with Deputy Boatright's mobile number. I texted Muriel's name and attached the photo with the Amygdalin prominently centered.

Mary Lu Scholl

CHAPTER 16

A NEW ENDING FOR MY BOOK

Was Muriel perspicacious enough to connect her break-in with her little pharmacy? Or did she consider herself safe; having been taken in and released?

I took an aspirin as my ankle had a dull ache with the occasional sharp pain but I decided I was not yet done for the night.

I texted the Deputy again that I was on my way over to make sure the drugs didn't disappear.

I got a message back in all capital letters. "DO NOT GO THERE! ON MY WAY."

I cringed as if he had shouted them right at me and sure enough my phone rang. I didn't answer him. I knew he just wanted to repeat himself. Waste of time, that. What made him think I wouldn't ignore a verbal warning if I was going to ignore a written one?

My slow, hobbling pace necessitated that I start out immediately; it was going to take me longer this time to get there, and sitting down had just made my ankle worse.

I was none too soon. Pete had his little truck-golf-cart backed up in her driveway. I hobbled past to a safe distance and waited. Several minutes passed.

Pete came out carrying a large cardboard box and set it in the back of his vehicle and went back in. I snapped a picture and sent it to the Deputy.

My phone rang and I ignored it again,

but Muriel was just coming out of her door with something else to add to the box. At the sound of my ringtone she looked sharply up.

"I should have known you'd be lurking about! Some kind of nosy Parker you are. Sticking your nose into everyone else's business! Lot of good it did you; I was cleared to come home and if they know what's what they'll be arresting you instead!"

Her voice carried stridently up and down the street. Even after dark there was no one at this end of the park who now didn't know I was there and Muriel was accusing me of murder.

I opened my mouth to answer back – because I'm just wired that way – and Pete came charging out of the door behind her. I didn't know what all she had told him, or how she explained the sudden urge to clean out her kitchen cabinets in the middle of the night. I also wasn't sure how she had convinced him it was important to help her in the middle of the night. Whatever she told him, he was almost as angry at my presence as she was.

With Pete for back-up she lost any inhibitions she might have otherwise had and she started crying and running toward me across the street, arms raised to attack.

I'm also wired for self-preservation, so I turned abruptly, and hurt my ankle yet again. I fell to the pavement and was barely getting back up when she reached me and nearly tripped herself as her momentum carried her into me. She had something hard in her hand and started hitting me on the head, pulling on my hair with the other hand.

I should have screamed, but it didn't even occur to me. I kept trying to get my feet under me as she tried to drag me towards the house and Pete.

He was standing there with his hands full and his mouth open. The cat-fight had him totally taken aback.

"Help me, Pete! We have to get rid of her! Help me get her in the house so we can…oomph…deal with her."

I got a good kick in that caused the oomph but my balance was compromised by my injury. The next thing I managed to grab was one of her feet and yank it out from under her as she was starting to step down on it. We landed in a pile of scratching, puffing and furious arms and legs.

I was briefly on top and slammed her head against the concrete. Pete dropped his box and finally headed into the fray.

He stopped at her side, lifting her head gently. With Muriel stunned, it was time for me to get out of there.

The Sheriff's vehicle pulled in and I

stopped when he stopped.

I made sure I was on the other side of the vehicle from the madwoman and her champion.

Pete had helped Muriel to her feet. She pushed her hair back away from her face and launched into a tirade about my harassing her and I had probably killed her Albert and what was he going to do about it?

She smoothed her dress and slid her foot back into the shoe that had flown off when I dumped her on her sorry ass. She did it smoothly and nonchalantly as if losing a shoe in the road in a cat fight happened all the time. Then she added that I had broken into her house and she was fortunate she hadn't been there or I would have killed her as well since my plan to frame her for poor Albert's death hadn't worked.

Deputy Boatright calmly waited until

she ran out of breath and stopped for air. She had a smudge of road dirt on her forehead. He frowned at me and told me not to go anywhere. He gently told her he was going to take care of everything and headed up her driveway. She had no choice but to follow him, even as she glared in my direction.

As they reached the golf cart, Muriel calmly addressed Pete. "I guess that's all the cleaning-out I have time for this evening. Thank you for helping me."

She stood aside, slightly in front of the Deputy to block him away from the path she wanted Pete and his cart to take – hopefully to the dumpster at the other end of the park if he could take a hint. Her chin indicated south on the street instead of towards the dumpster right behind us.

Pete picked up the box he had dropped and put it in the cargo area of his little vehicle.

Deputy Boatright raised a hand to stop Pete's compliance. "You've been busy." He addressed the still irate, but now also nervous woman beside him.

"I've decided to clear out a lot of unnecessary clutter from when my late husband was ill." She raised her face defiantly in my direction but directed her words toward Pete and the Deputy. "When her man is first passed," she looked down demurely, "there are a lot of things a widow just can't get rid of; as time passes it gets a little easier to let go."

"This whole episode has shown me that it is past time to get on with my life." She continued as she smiled at Pete and wiped non-existent tears from the corner of her eyes.

"So what exactly is in those boxes? Do you mind if I take a look?" The deputy raised an eyebrow in apparent casual inquiry.

Muriel hesitated and Pete jumped to

her defense. "Do you have a search warrant?"

I guessed that he was declaring love over blood-by-marriage as he chose which side to support.

Deputy Boatright took out his phone and punched in a few numbers. As he waited for an answer he questioned Muriel. "Do I need one?"

Before she could answer there was a voice answering him from his phone.

"This is Deputy Boatright. Is the search warrant for Muriel Johnson's home, vehicle and person approved?"

There was an answer, albeit not loud enough for us to hear. "Thank you. We'll wait for you to bring it."

"Did you want us all to wait inside, Mrs. Johnson? Pete, are you staying or do you have something else to do?"

Last chance. The Deputy Detective seemed to be giving him a last chance to get out of the fire.

Pete was thoughtful for a full moment. Then he edged carefully past Muriel. "We can finish this tomorrow, Muriel. Call me in the morning." He unloaded the boxes from his little cart-truck and nodded at Deputy Boatright and glared at me.

What did I do?

"Mrs. Decker, why don't you go home and wait for me to get back to you. Try to stay out of trouble between here and there. Don't leave the park." The detective deputy raised that supercilious eyebrow again.

CHAPTER 17

EPILOGUE

It was a blessing not to be in a hurry for once that night. I stopped at the laundry/lavatory on the way. I looked at my reflection and wondered whether I was the only one who had weathered a tornado.

Then I noticed that as many times as I changed the toilet paper in the laundry/shower room, someone always changed it back. There was now a sticky note on the wall above the roller.

To whom it may concern. This park's

committee has voted to comply with the manufacturer's and Ann Lander's instructions on how to hang this paper. Please abide by this decision.

I would have to come back later with a pen and write "No." For the moment. I just reversed the way it was hanging.

Once home (when did it get to be that?) I realized that I was hungry. Well, not hungry, nervous. Same thing in the long run; so I grabbed one of the breakfast burritos I routinely made ahead and kept in the freezer. I stuck it in the microwave while I changed my now dirty and torn clothes.

I pulled the burrito out and burned my hand. I wrapped a paper towel around it. I realized I had taken my teeth out when I walked up the steps, force of habit. I put my teeth back in. *All the easier to eat a burrito with, Grandma.*

Then I sat down to wait. I tried to concentrate on my knitting while I waited but had to un-knit practically every row as soon as I got to the end and realized I had jumped rows on the pattern. I finally threw the whole thing into my knitting bag and tossed it into a corner.

Albert had popped in, taken one look at my expression and popped back out.

Smart ghost, that Albert.

Then I decided to make cookies. Fortunately they required no thought and I was taking a batch of flourless peanut butter – chocolate chip cookies out of the little oven as the Deputy pulled up and parked.

He was alone. Either that woman had talked her way out of trouble or I had been too late and the Amygdalin was already gone.

"Shall I come in or are you coming out?" He asked companionably.

"I'll come out. Would you like a warm cookie?"

"Is it safe to eat?"

"I'm not the one with the foreign pharmacy." I joined him on the porch and waved him toward the glider as I hooked Buddy on his chain, set the cookies just out of Buddy's reach, and sat in a folding chair. "Peanut butter and chocolate chip, gluten free if you care. Sugar, though." I took one and gave a bite to Buddy anyway.

"Do I want to know why you're limping?" He asked me. Then his attention went to his cookie. "This is good."

Albert was suddenly in the other folding chair.

"You don't have to look so surprised, you know. I am a good cook. And, no; you don't want to know why I'm limping." I took a bite and then added. "Besides that, I'm old and everything hurts. I don't remember why my ankle hurts."

Albert rolled his eyes at me. That's a reaction usually attributed to teenagers, and girls far more often than boys. It was neither childish or feminine on him, though.

"So, the picture you sent, when did you take it? When you were visiting the other day, or earlier this evening?"

"I was looking through my gallery pictures and noticed it. I take a lot of pictures."

Now Albert was just shaking his head. If he made me laugh, so help me…

"Off the record, since you have been so helpful, I'll tell you that Muriel admitted to giving him the Amygdalin in the muffin she gave him. She was trying to save him the pain and degradation – as she put it – of a lingering illness. I suspect she was also trying to save herself the lingering pain as she would be unwilling to abandon her friendship, but also was unwilling to provide the caregiving she would feel bound to offer."

"That last is just my take on it, she didn't say so in so many words." Deputy Boatright then got back to business.

"Now. About the definition of stalking." He started and then stopped at my expression. "I've accidentally deleted the picture you sent me. In asking for the search warrant I referred to an anonymous tip confirming a suspicion we already had after analyzing the medications found in Mr. Cross' house."

"Law enforcement can be dangerous and you have demonstrated a serious lack of boundaries. I hope in the future you can enjoy retirement. Take up weaving pine needle baskets or something. Leave any more dead bodies to us to sort out."

Properly chastened, I made a promise that was sincere when I made it.

After all, what were the chances of having another neighbor drop dead?

(Pretty good, actually.) For an excerpt from Mobile Mayhem →

MOBILE MAYHEM

Sally was selling the cards (which are no longer cards but sheets of paper specially printed for the semi-professional Bingo crowd) and I had already purchased two ink daubers from a discount store so we each had one to use.

The program had barely launched when a man bustled into the room and up to his wife.

The caller was miffed and stopped the game. There were boos and hisses from the previously "ruly" crowd, now becoming "unruly."

"Well?" Demanded Martha, impatiently. "What is so all-fired important that it couldn't wait?"

"The Sheriff's Office started searching for Henry a couple of hours ago and found him in the woods to the west of the park." The informant held his breath for a dramatic pause. "Dead."

I looked down at the sheet I had been slowly completing. The red splotches on the light blue numbers now reminded me of bloody fingerprints.

Pandemonium broke out.

* * *

Gossip had started immediately. It was absolutely amazing the number of gospel truths that were held forth from the little bit of real information they had gotten.

Suddenly everyone knew how he had died. They didn't. Suddenly everyone knew what he was doing in the woods. They didn't. Suddenly it was murder and everyone knew who did it. Jessica's daughter.

Somehow, and with no surprise, Justine had managed to alienate everyone in the park with the same ease with which she breathed.

She had been rude to a Good Samaritan, Ralph. She had been rude to a protected young member of the community, Lucy. She had been accusatory toward the respected manager, Jeremiah. She was dismissive and unconcerned about her mother. Lastly, she had been abusive toward a well-liked, deceased (and thereby imbued with saintly qualities) resident, Henry.

It was only in our own small company that I pointed out quite reasonably that as much as I would love to blame her, she hadn't even shown up until well after Henry's disappearance.

Not my problem, this time. I was not going to get involved.

Please consider leaving me a review on Amazon or on Goodreads. Reviews are our lifeblood as authors!

Find me at:
https://www.amazon.com/author/maryluscholl

ABOUT THE AUTHOR

Mary Lu Scholl kissed the Blarney Stone and has never looked back.
Retired and living in the paradise of West Central Florida, on the Nature Coast, she writes cozy mysteries for both men and women. She lives with her mom and a cat, around the corner from her daughter. Family is steadily migrating toward the warm climate and she looks forward to having everyone close.

TRAILER PARK TRAVAILS
PATTY DECKER COZY MYSTERIES

Camper Catastrophe (Book 1)

www.amazon.com/dp/B07MHV48PH

Mobile Mayhem (Book 2)

www.amazon.com/dp/B07MWBL8P

Birds, Bees and RVs (Book 3)

www.amazon.com/dp/B07PM8Z35H

Trailer Trauma (Book 4)

www.amazon.com/dp/B07YCSS9GS

Modular Murder (Book 5)

www.amazon.com/dp/B084T817MG

Corpse in the Clubhouse (Book 6)

www.amazon.com/dp/B08NJ6B2WF

Restless Retirement (Book 7)

www.amazon.com/dp/B093FWNRGY

Soon! Motorhome Motives (Book 8)

www.amazon.com/dp/B09CP1FF29

Eventually, Patty encounters Bernie
Murphy.
Bernie lives nearby and that's where
Nature Coast Calamities pick up.
With a hint of Irish Folklore,

NATURE COAST CALAMITIES

BERNIE MURPHY COZY MYSTERIES

Lecanto Leprechaun (Book 1)

www.amazon.com/dp/B09ZKNVL49

Big Foot and the Bentley (Book 2)

www.amazon.com/dp/B0B7QHJKM2

InverNessie (Book 3)

www.amazon.com/dp/B0BCHCSX3B

And – coming up soon - a story about manatees, mermaids and murder!

Made in United States
North Haven, CT
31 January 2024

48148848R00104